Trash to Treasure

A Good Tale

Volume 1

A Good Tale
Volume 1

Trash to Treasure

An Anthology project of the LinkedIn Fiction Writers Guild

Unexpected Treasure © 2014 Harry Alexiou

What Becomes © 2014 Tim Girard

3 D T. C. © 2014 Mike Boggia

Dragon Bones © 2014 Joseph Scott Amis

The Birthday Present © 2014 By A. A. Abbott

Baby Rose © 2014 Lynette White

Bookends © 2014 Allen Quintana

The Treasure of Freedom © 2014 Randall Lemon

City Business © 2014 Patricia Lovett

Life Race © 2014 Alli Vaughan

Dino Planetarium © 2014 Sylvia Stein

An Empty Box of Treasure © 2014 Rejoice Denhere

Of Dinosaurs and Girls © 2014 by Laura Stafford

Boredom © 2014 by D. C. Mills

Expressing Ourselves © 2014 by Douglas G. Clarke

Cover by Julianna Putri, Juliannaputri on fiverr.com

Contact the publisher at, support@agoodtale.com

First Printing, 2014

ISBN 978-1-63427-003-8

To all the authors:
Who accept the challenge each month to write a story based on someone else's prompt
Who take a few unrelated thoughts and turn them into their own
Who thrill us with adventure
Who bring a tear to our eyes or a chuckle and a smile
Who, with about a thousand words, entertain us for a few minutes

To all the authors, new and old, experienced and just starting out, who share their stories with each other each month.

To the authors who decided to include their stories here, to those who choose to pursue other opportunities, and to those who write for themselves.

This book is dedicate to you in thanks for being part of the group.

Table of Contents

Introduction

Trash to Treasure is a collection of short stories resulting from the question, "What do a dinosaur, a pawnshop and graffiti have in common?"

Sixteen authors took up the challenge and went in different directions. From the despair of a life that has sunk so low that a pawnshop is the only option, to the treasures to be found in one. From visiting a park that celebrates all that dinosaurs were, to life as one. From graffiti as a reflection of poverty and desperation, to an art form.

Join us as we look at how trash can be transformed into treasure, physically and metaphorically.

Unexpected Treasure

by Harry Alexiou

Mary allowed the tears to spill freely as she stood in front of their house, or at least it had been their house. The low white picket fence had long been flattened, scattered pieces remained, enough to evoke happy memories of tending to the lawn, and to the roses; they had brought much needed colour and fragrance to the street. The façade of the house had been heartlessly vandalised, windows smashed, now boarded up, and multi-coloured graffiti in place of once lovingly restored paintwork. Tommy tugged at his mother's coat as he looked up to her, his dark brown eyes holding a light frown.

"Mum, what happened to our house?"

She wiped her eyes and knelt down in front of him, still unable to tell him the truth about their former family home and of his father's tragic demise.

"Tommy, this isn't ours anymore. We sold it and that's why we're living with Uncle Peter."

"But Ian at school sold his house and they got money and bought another house."

Mary searched her fragile mind for a way to explain to him. He was too young to understand about world recession, negative equity and bad loans. She wouldn't burden him with the realities of the new world order – where formerly affluent middle class families suddenly found themselves without jobs and without homes. She couldn't tell him about the many desperate souls who'd been unable to provide for their families and had taken their own lives, including his dad. She hugged her son and felt his beating heart against hers; one day soon she would tell him the truth.

Little Tommy pushed away, his eyes wide; "Can we go inside mum?"

"No Tommy, I don't think -"

"Please mum, can I see my old room?"

Mary checked the time and glanced up and down the quiet road; they had 15 minutes until the bus arrived.

"Come on then, let's see if the side gate is open."

The pair approached the house and pushed aside the tall weeds to get to the entrance. The rusty hinges creaked halfway open and they pushed their way in. Tommy held his mother's hand tighter than ever and threw an anxious look over his shoulder.

The garden was so overgrown Mary couldn't differentiate between the edge of the grass and the flower beds. One object she hoped would still be there, amongst the dereliction, was that special rock, the one which reminded her of a small tortoise. She brushed away dead leaves, and flattened weeds searching with unexpected verve. Her heart skipped as her fingers touched a cold hard object and she uncovered the stone; a tiny part of her did cartwheels as the hidden silver key, wrapped in clear plastic, glinted in the light. Tommy grinned and followed his mother as she opened up the backdoor.

The stink of wet rot hit them as it escaped from the confines of the shuttered property. They entered, and all the memories flew at Mary, her stomach churning as the melancholy fixed itself inside her. Hesitant at first, she followed Tommy's lead as he rushed ahead, up the staircase, illuminated by a small window halfway up.

Mary heard a commotion as she entered his old room. Tommy sat on the floor looking at an ugly stone statue of a dinosaur which his dad had given him. She'd hoped never to see it again and forgot she'd hidden it away the day they'd moved out.

Since losing almost everything, Mary had become rather more inquisitive of people's junk and the items discarded by others. She studied the intricate ornament with a more discerning eye than she would have six months ago.

"Let me hold onto the statue Tommy, just in case you drop it. Now have a quick look around, then we really must leave."

The bus arrived and Mary paid for the ride to the high street; they had one more stop before going back to her brother's house.

Mary held the dinosaur tight and turned to her son as he tapped her arm.

"Dad bought me the dinosaur, I remember."

"Yes that's right sweetheart, and I'm sure it's worth some money. We're going to the shop with all the old stuff, to see how much we can get."

"Mum, where is dad?"

The unexpected question stabbed at her heart and she diverted her gaze.

"He's gone away to find a job."

"When is he coming back?"

"Oh… quick, this is our stop Tommy." The timing was perfect as she stood and grabbed his hand.

The pawnbroker turned the statue upside down then weighed it up and down in his hand. He placed it on the counter and flicked through a well thumbed catalogue, settling on a page.

"Yeah thought so, these were made in their hundreds of thousands back in the day when dinosaur movies were the ones to watch. It's worthless...sorry luv." He handed it back to her.

"Are you sure? Please check again."

"No need to, sorry I couldn't help."

They exited the shop. Mary was stunned by the man's comments, and his trampling on her morsel of hope. She glanced down at Tommy.

"It's all yours Tommy...Not worth anything."

"But mum, dad gave me this. I have to look after it, and when he comes back, I'm going tell him that it was lost, but I found it… like lost treasure!"

Mary smiled and stroked the back of his head. "That's a lovely thought Tommy."

What Becomes

by Tim Girard

Quiet tonight, on the streets. Downtown. I'm tired. I feel old. The weight of the world sits on my shoulders as I lumber along, too worn out to be bitter, too overwhelmed to care about much.

I lost my way. Somehow. I don't know where. If I did, I would walk back in and demand it back. But I can't so now I just walk the streets when I should be at home. With my family. Only my family sees my pain, sees the broken tooth of my failure. I can't be the man I am supposed to be and they know it. My children don't respect me. They order me about like some sort of hired help.

I laugh at the thought. Someone has a job at least. The hired help.

My wife won't look at me without the sticky tar of disgust. It gets on my feet and I am mired.

It's been so long since I kissed a woman; I think about crying.

I am so lonely.

I pass a toy shop. Then a pawn shop. Then a grocery store. They have things I want in there. Toys for my kids. Nice things for my wife. My arms hang at my sides. They are useless and I know it.

I try to remember what she looked like when we were young, but my feet are too big and I just trample through the brush.

I look over at the flotsams laying together. I wonder what brought them out, huddled as they are. One of them eyes me and I snap my teeth trying to be menacing. He snorts and puts his head down and closes his eyes. Figures.

I think about stomping over to him and roaring in his face, but I hold my rage. It wouldn't serve any purpose, but to scratch my throat and my heels are protesting enough tonight thank you very much.

I let him sleep. I think of him as a him, you see. It makes me feel strong. If I called him a her I would be admitting my impotence and I am not really in the mood to do that. Maybe another time. Call me?

I pause at the expansive park before me. I could find sleep here. I could, but the thought of laying out in the open has no appeal to me. I watch the wind blow a shopping bag across the grass.

"I know how you feel!" I shout, then I feel stupid for being so loud. Someone tells me to shut up. No one cares.

You should care! You'll hear about me! I ain't done yet!

It almost sounds good. I almost believe it myself, the graffiti stains of my angst scrawled across my bewilderment. They know how empty it is. So do I.

Cleansing breath. A big sigh. Close your eyes. Count to ten. Heck, make it eleven. What's one more gonna hurt?

My tummy rumbles and I feel small for calling it a tummy. Maybe someday I'll eat again. Maybe.

Overhead a comet streaks bright across the sky.

Great. I wonder what that means.

3 D T. C.

by Mike Boggia

T. C. dropped the spray paint can into his backpack and walked across the street. This time he executed the painting to perfection. The Triple Globe Pawnshop's east wall sported a rich, Jurassic flora mural. Front and center a Kaatedocus grinned back at him. The dinosaur's clever camouflage colors hid it in the trees and bushes. The beast was easy to overlook, if one did not study the painting with care.

On the birth certificate, his given name was John D. Smith. He never knew a father. His mother claimed to be a nightclub singer and slept days. As he grew older, graffiti was his means of flipping his finger at the world and life.

Art became an obsession under the guidance of his junior high art instructor. Ms. Springer recognized talent and encouraged it. Without money for supplies, he liberated spray paint cans wherever he found them. His style of painting, one can in each hand, earned him the nickname Two Cans, or T. C. among local graffiti artists.

Best one I've done. I hope old man Muter leaves it alone. He lounged against the second hand store's wall and grinned. The street light cast a surreal glow, which brought the jungle to life. An overwhelming sensation told him that if he crossed the narrow street he could walk inside the mural.

Sirens screamed nearby. Snapped back to reality, the fourteen year old flattened himself against the wall, sucked in his breath and waited. The sound faded. He shouldered his pack and slunk through the shadows.

Midway across a deserted street, headlights blinded him. He froze, and then ran as red and blue lights wig wagged. Propelled by fear, he fled back the way he had come, a cop in pursuit.

He'd been busted before and performed community service twice. Judge Heller warned him that next time he'd send the teenager to juvenile detention.

T. C. turned down the alley between the pawnshop and second hand store. He slipped and reeled into the painting, hands extended. Impact never occurred; instead, he stumbled over a vine and landed against a cycad. Grassy breath warmed his face. He looked up into the toothy smile of the Kaatedocus. It sniffed the visor of his cap, sneezed, and continued grazing.

T. C. curled up against the trunk of a tree fern and slept. A garbage truck rumbled through the alley, waking him. He peered at the world beyond his jungle and contemplated staying within the safety of its boundaries.

On the sidewalk, across the street, Mr. Muter's angry voice argued with a well-dressed man, who gestured toward the painting.

"It is garbage, trash, this thing you call a treasure." Muter stamped his foot. "It is my shop and I will paint over this graffiti no matter what you say, Mr. Hubbard." He turned to the painters standing behind him, and jabbed his forefinger at their compressor. "Cover that damnable, hideous clash of color."

"No," Hubbard protested. "Let me take pictures. I need to locate the artist."

"Vandal!" Muter's face flushed a shade of dark fuchsia. "If you pay for painting my wall, you can take all the pictures you want."

Hubbard wrote a check and handed it to Muter. He removed a camera from his briefcase and snapped photos. "I really think you should leave it alone."

Muter shouted expletives and ordered the painters to start spraying.

T. C. realized if he stayed hidden, he'd be trapped inside the painting. He burst out of the undergrowth onto the sidewalk and collided with Hubbard.

The man grabbed his arm. "I swear you just came…no, wait." He examined the paint on T. C.'s fingers and looked back at the graffiti. "Are you the artist?"

"You gonna call the cops?"

"Young man, the paint on your fingers matches the paint on the wall."

"I did it, okay. Lemme go."

"Not so fast. My name is Joseph H. Hubbard, owner of Hubbard and Hubbard Galleria. You're wasting your talent. Your street art needs to be seen and not be considered graffiti."

"Yeah, sure." T. C. attempted to pull away.

"I own several buildings in the warehouse district. The city is trying to rejuvenate that locale and your paintings would serve a dual purpose. It will bring color to the area and further your experience as an artist in a legitimate manner."

T. C. stopped struggling. "You want me to paint for you?"

"I do. I'll provide paint and pay you for the murals. We can discuss price according to size with your parents. There's one condition. You must stay in school and graduate."

He studied the art dealer, who offered his hand.

"For real?"

"For real, my word of honor." Hubbard shook the boy's hand.

Behind T. C., Kaatedocus winked.

Dragon Bones

by Joseph Scott Amis

November 26, 1092, Southeastern France

Knight Thierré de Coudre stood and pulled his cloak over his shoulders. He looked at his younger brother. "Are you coming with me or not?"

Galien picked up his own cloak. "I suppose so, but I don't think it wise. If the Bishop's men arrest us we'll end up in deep cells."

"To hell with the Bishop's men. They'll need answer to this if they bother us." Thierré drew his sword. The blade gleamed in the firelight as he flashed his wicked grin. "I trust you've your own at ready hand?"

"I have, but I'm not near so eager to draw it."

Alisende de Coudre stepped into the room. "Surely you two aren't going out to drink on a night like this."

Thierré smiled at her. "Dear sister, you know that a little wind and sleet never keep Galien and me from adventure. We're going to explore the chemist's house before the Bishop has it torn down."

"I've always wondered what that old wizard kept hidden in there. I'm coming with you."

"Sister, this isn't for girls."

"Shut up, bigmouth." Alisende took her twelve-inch dagger from the wall and stuck it in her belt. "I'm coming, and that is that."

The brothers grinned at each other. Galien said, "We've learned not to cross you when your mind is made up. Fetch your cloak and let's go."

* * *

Two guards wearing the Bishop's colors stood before the chemist's house. Thierré walked up to them, hand on his sword hilt. "Stand aside. We would enter."

"Sir de Coudre, all know full well that His Eminence has declared this to be unholy ground. We won't try to stop you, but you enter at risk of your soul."

"You can tell His Eminence that I call his declaration hogwash. I'm only glad that my father took issue before your master could execute a harmless and dying old man."

The guard nodded. "Even His Eminence dares not contend with Henri de Coudre. But in truth the chemist was a necromancer."

"More humbug from that scoundrel you call a Bishop. Now move aside!"

* * *

The oaken front door screeched on rusted hinges as Thierré pushed it open. Galien sparked a torch and they crept in with caution. As they explored the ground and second floors, the torchlight revealed only shabby rooms, broken furniture, and papers and objects scattered in chaos. Thierré turned round and shrugged. "No surprise that the good Bishop's henchmen were here well before us. Can this be all?"

"There's yet the cellar, brother," Galien said.

"Then lead us there."

Thierré and Alisende followed Galien down a steep flight of rickety steps to the dank cellar. Galien walked around. "This was surely his laboratory."

Thierré's spine prickled and he shivered in spite of himself. "From the way it smells down here, the Bishop might have been right about the old man."

"Come quickly. I see something!" Alisende pointed to a wall stacked with furniture and Galien held out the torch. "There's writing on the wall."

Galien handed her the torch, then he and Thierré moved a heavy cupboard aside. Thierré traced a finger over the scrawled Latin. "Can you read it, brother?"

"Not offhand, but find me something to write with. I'll copy it and we'll go back to father's house."

"The sooner the better," Thierré said. "This place reeks of evil deeds."

* * *

Galien sat at the table before the fire, books open before him. Thierré and Alisende stood by and sipped cups of wine, in silent awe as their scholarly brother meticulously translated the words into French. Galien looked up. "Done!"

Thierré took a long swallow of wine. "What are you waiting for? Read it to us."

Galien held the parchment up and read aloud:

"In ancient times the dragons gathered at their homeland in the far land of Var.

Men waged war against them and they departed, some say on great wings to the far north beyond the sea, others say that they were cast forever into Hell.

But their burial grounds remain, and the knight that drinks a potion made of the bones will never fall in battle.

Bravest of knights, be warned. The dragon spirits stand guard there, and only the most blessed might prevail against them.

Thierré snorted and said, "More hogwash. Dragons are but old folktales," and Alisende, "Thank you for the interesting evening, brothers, but I'm nearly ready to fall asleep where I stand."

* * *

Galien and Thierré crawled into their beds in the second floor chamber. Thierré looked over. "Galien, in truth, what do think?"

"I've also thought dragons only legend, but together we've seen that folktales can turn out to be true. And if we found those bones we could make a fortune."

"Hmm. Is there really a place called Var?"

"Yes, near the southeast coast and toward Germany. It's been known since Roman times and before."

Thierré stroked his chin. "Our next job is in Lyon. How far does Var lie from there?"

"A hard four day ride."

"That's nothing for us. We can kill the vampire for the Bishop of Lyon in short time and take an easy five day ride to Var."

"Brother, we've not yet faced a vampire, but they're no easy kills. And if it bites you, you turn into one."

"Blast. After killing the witch and her army of living corpses, I thought one vampire would be easy."

Galien patted the ancient book on the small table between the beds. "It won't be easy, but if we follow what's written in here we can do it."

"Brother, I can only thank God that you learned letters as well as you did."

"And there's no better swordsman than you. In our line of work, we can't do without each other."

"Then we're ready for that vampire and those dragon bones, but now we both need some sleep. Snuff out the candle, will you?"

The Birthday Present

By A.A. Abbott

Usually you'd never go there. You're used to paying your way. Don't have a credit card, won't touch the payday lenders. But that's before Big Archie comes round.

"Your Kian owes me money," he says.

You protest that it's nothing to do with you. Kian's your younger brother; you're not his keeper. He's skedaddled to London, probably in prison for all you know.

"That's a shame, because you wouldn't want anything to happen to that pretty lass of yours, or the bairn, would you?" he asks with a nasty smile. He's holding one of your Timmy's ferrets, the white one called Snowy. He's stroking it at first, then all of a sudden, he breaks its neck. Just like that.

You drew the dole this morning, so you give it all to Big Archie, or at least all but the ten pounds Lisa just took to the shops. The looming Archie problem is solved, but now you've got some different ones. Like how to explain to

Lisa that the food she's bought today has to last two weeks. And where to hide the dead ferret before she returns with Timmy.

The hill is a rising sweep of handsome redbrick Georgian houses. It looks like it should be grand, but a stew it was 200 years ago, and a stew it remains today. The pawnbrokers, Brunners, isn't one of the brash, flash new chains. It's been there, tucked away, for decades, unnoticed by all save those who need it. They take your wedding ring, the pressure cooker and the boxed purple dinosaur you were going to give Timmy for his birthday. The small amount of cash they give you is criminal. Now you know why the graffiti outside says 'legal loan sharks.'

Timmy notices Snowy's gone AWOL. He bawls his eyes out. You tell him it was too hot for Snowy, so the ferret ran away to the North Pole. He believes you. You were gullible too when you weren't quite three years old.

"Why aren't you wearing your ring?" Lisa wants to know.

"I've lost weight and it keeps falling off."

She doesn't miss the pressure cooker at first. Once she does, the whole story comes out and there's hell to pay. After the screaming stops, she tells you to get the dinosaur back. "I'm still paying fifty pence a week to my catalogue for that," she says. "We've promised the bairn a purple dinosaur for his birthday and it'll break his heart if he doesn't get one."

You've got a week before his birthday. This time, you take your iPod to Brunners. They're interested, but the dinosaur's gone. "Put it in the window and it sold straight away," they tell you. You can have the pressure cooker, though, and ten pounds in cash. As for the wedding ring, who knows how long you'll stay married, anyway?

So now you've got ten pounds for a dinosaur, but nobody's selling purple ones any more: not the catalogue, not Argos, not the sad old-fashioned toy shop that scrapes by at the top of the hill. "Do you want a red one?" they ask hopefully. No wonder it didn't stay in Brunners' window for long.

Lisa starts asking all her friends if anyone's seen a purple dinosaur for sale. No, they haven't, but someone's seen an old one in Big Archie's front garden.

She sends you round to look. She says to wear dark glasses, but he'll know it's you, so you don't bother. Maybe there's a glint of purple in the corner of that concrete-slabbed space, underneath the broken TVs and pizza boxes and beer cans. Nothing living grows there. Even the weeds are afraid.

Big Archie's lass, Stella, is standing outside with a cigarette. Funny, who would have thought he was so particular about smoking inside his house?

"His lordship doesn't wish to be disturbed," she says. "Sleeping off a hangover."

You poke at the garbage where you glimpsed purple plastic. Yes, it's there. "Can I take that?" you ask, pointing to the dinosaur.

"You certainly can. It's been nothing but trouble to us. Archie saw it in Brunners' window, said he always wanted one and brought it back. He starts on the weed, and goodness knows what else, watches a film and then he's screaming about T Rex wanting to eat him. I ask you, does this place look like Jurassic Park?"

"What did you do?" You're curious. The lives of Big Archie and his bird sound like one of the soaps Lisa likes to watch when Timmy's asleep.

"Threw this miserable piece of plastic out here and gave him a beer. It was either that or the Bible, and Archie can't read."

There's a commotion behind her as Big Archie bursts through the door. He lours over her, broad as a house, eyes wild. You know he has an opinion to air, and that's never good. "You can't have that," he yells at you. "Me mam promised me one of those when I was a lad; never gave it to me. "

You're not surprised. Everyone knows his mam's first and only love was a vodka bottle.

"I want that thing out of my house," Stella says, stubbing out her cigarette on the front wall.

He takes a swing at her, but she ducks and catches him a clout to the jaw.

She shrugs. "You're going soft, big man. I'm out of here."

"Me too," you say.

"Give that back," he says to you.

You've taken the precaution of moving twenty yards away from him. You might need a head start. "Are you sure?" you ask. "You wouldn't want the whole town to know your lass was clashing you, would you?"

His broad shoulders slump. "Get out," he spits. "I never want to see your ugly face again."

That suits you just fine. You take Timmy's present home to wrap.

Baby Rose

by Lynette White

It just never seemed to get better for Rose. Two years ago she lost her mother to cancer and one month to the day after that her husband Derrick was killed in a car accident.

She squeaked by after Derrick's death until three months ago when she was dealt another crippling blow. She was laid off from her job and could not find another one.

With tears in her blue eyes she stopped in front of the local pawn shop. It's green exterior with intentional graffiti 'for character' stood in sharp contrast to the buildings around it. Unfortunately it was the only stable business now days.

Everyone seemed to be in the same situation she was except for the buyers who frequented the pawn shop. With no remorse they bought up everything of value just to sell it elsewhere for a huge profit.

Rose straightened her shoulders, tossed back her long blonde hair and wiped away the tears with the back of the hand that held one of her grandmother's paintings. Grasping her other hand was her son Devon.

He was only three and already a spitting image of Derrick from his unruly brown hair to his long legs. Rose forced a smile as she looked down at her son, the most treasured gift Derrick ever gave her.

He looked up and mimicked her smile as if to encourage her. In his other hand was he favorite stuffed dinosaur, a gift from his dad just one week before he left for work, never to come home.

"Alright little man, I need you to be really good while I talk to the people in here."

Devon's eyes screwed up in distaste as they scanned the building in front of them. "I don't like this place, mommy. It always makes you cry."

She leaned over and kissed him on the forehead. "It is not this place that makes me cry, baby. Sometimes we have to do things we don't like, but when I am done we will go the store and buy something nice for dinner. I will even buy your favorite cereal, ok?

Devon squeezed his stuffed dinosaur tighter and his little face was just a little brighter. "Ok, mommy."

She took a deep breath and moved toward the door. She hated the idea of pawning what little she had to keep a roof over their head. She felt a little better when she saw Gary talking to another man. Gary owned the pawn shop and was always good to her.

He was an older man with a rough exterior, but a big heart. He was round in the middle and nearly bald, but Gary was tougher than he looked.

Both men looked at her as she entered, on the counter was a sketch they were apparently discussing. The other man was smartly dressed and about Gary's age with coal black hair streaked with gray.

"Rose, Devon, how are you today." Gary greeted her with a big smile.

"I'm fine, Gary." She answered with a shaky voice. "I have a couple of things I would like to sell, please."

The other man nodded and so Gary left him too tend to Rose. "What you got, Rose?"

She glanced down at her wedding ring, that would wait. She placed the painting on the counter. "I have this painting my grandmother did. I have four more and my mother told me they were the last ones grandmother painted."

The other man moved closer and his eyes widened as he looked at the painting. "Dear God, is this what I think it is?"

He looked at Rose. "You said your grandmother painted this?"

Rose gulped. "Yes, and my mother told me they were of me."

"What is your name?"

"Rose…Rose Cassidy." She stammered and looked at Gary for some help.

"This is David Simmons, he is an art collector friend of mine." Gary offered.

Rose nodded. "I see, pleased to meet you."

"And you." David said with a nod. "What was your grandmother's name?"

Rose hesitated. "Carolyn Jackson."

He picked up the painting and examined it closely. "Gary, this is not only a Carolyn Jackson original, but the Baby Rose series was indeed the last one she painted."

His mouth dropped as he put the pieces together. "You must be baby Rose."

"I…I…guess so. She died when I was Devon's age."

"Do you have any idea what this painting is worth?"

"No sir."

"The other four painting in this series sold for over $10,000 each, and since her unexpected death, they've resold for three times that. Rumors said there were more in the series, but no one expected to ever see a new paining from her; I know some very prestigious auction houses who would love to see this painting, and the others."

Rose stumbled back, face slack, unable to breath. She looked to Gary.

Gary nodded his agreement. "Not to mention that Rose is every bit as talented with the brush as Carolyn was."

Rose blushed as David's eyes lit up. "Is that true Rose?"

"I … I guess so," she stammered.

David pointed at Gary. "I've know Gary a long time and he's never steered me wrong. If he thinks you've got what it takes, I'd be stupid not to listen." David pulled out his checkbook, filled one out, and handed it to Rose.

Devon pulled on her arm so he could read it, "$7,000." The memo line read, "Advance on future paintings."

Bookends

by Allen Quintana

The old pawnshop shared a wall with a clothing store on one side that catered to over-the-hill hippies harkening for their long lost groove. On the other, a fancy and faded marquis read "Music" atop that establishment, as passers-by could hear from within the occasional piano-plinking of its students, favoring classical over contemporary.

The addresses of these businesses and others, were overlooked by most patrons of this dark city of too many, being off the beaten paths of the newer and wider thoroughfares that bypassed these old, established storefronts.

Their owners lived from day to day in their livelihoods; living and breathing their expertise, decades in the making, completely missed by the younger and out of touch.

Still these older merchants' establishments faired and functioned for the special niche of folk who knew of their hidden treasures and wares which were cheaper and better than what was found in the fancy malls whose shoppers cared only for buying the name on the product. And those clueless would do it again, paying through the nose for the latest fad emblazoned on its cheaply-made imports and knock-offs.

The street and stores had seen better days – many of those ago; now dilapidated and worn. Even the graffiti was faded in the alleyways; their authors either grown up or passed on.

Small signs of "for sale" or "for lease" were in abundance and unnoticed. Despite the "steals" a customer could get here, there was hardly anything that looked worth taking from these grey and grimy, exhaust-encrusted edifices. Yet livelihoods continued in this forgotten borough.

A small brass bell ting-a-linged as the door to the pawnshop jarred. A tall figure stepped over its threshold and the shadow of the man became one with the dimness of the store.

He stopped and took it in.

The pawnshop was filled with a collage of collectibles and artifacts and antiques. Knickknacks filled its nooks and crannies. To his right, a box overflowed with folded and faded front pages of newspapers headlining something or 'nother. In a beat up bin to his left leaned jacketed records of big bands and symphonies – deserving to be rediscovered.

The shop smelled of old; a musty, stilled presence that belied the history of its walls and its wares, which deserved such a place. Somewhere a radio etched in a tinny din, a quiet show tune that was in keeping with what was hung, stacked, shelved, and stored here with the old things and the dust.

A small, but impressive, wooden roll-top desk was tucked against the back of the store. Seated at it was the store owner, nose buried in a book.

"Hi, Bridget," the man said. "What's new?"

The man could only tell the woman's head turned to-and-fro by the slight shake of her rangy gray hair. She then lifted her gaze in his direction.

"Really, Hank," sounding as if she was about to lecture an unruly youth, "If you're going to throw out some one-liners, I have some better reads in the "Humor" section."

"Just seeing what's—come in since last time."

"Hmm," Bridget said. "I suppose I shouldn't be surprised." Her accent evoked images of burgermeisters and rugged, snow-capped peaks. She took a bookmark from a cup filled with others priced to sell, placing it in her book and set the read in one of the roll-tops' pigeon holes.

"You know, Hank," she mused, "I have something you might like. It's "Bernhardt's Fossil Guide", final edition. Very good shape."

"And very out of date," Hank countered. "Besides, he was wrong about a few things."

"Quite the coffee table book. Give you a good price." Bridget flashed a toothy smile.

"Uh, uh," her friend smiled back. "Coming for the usual."

Bridget shrugged and led Hank to the back of the store. A generous portion of it contained shelf upon shelf of dusty, dog-eared, cloth-covered or leather bound, small and oversized, old and older, first-edition books.

"Thank you, my friend. I'll let you know when I'm done."

"Of course," Bridget returned the nod dutifully. "Just yell if you need anything else." She adjusted a leather-bound volume that was slightly out of place then walked back to her roll-top.

Bridget observed in her years of ownership that sound carried well in her shop, and that included the quiet gasp or breathy exclamation when something was newly discovered. She smiled at Hank's and the quick, anxious pace of footsteps on creaky floorboards that came her way. She looked up. "Yes?"

Hank had an astonished look on his face. He held up an object in each hand, is eyes seemingly as large the grapefruit-sized egg-shaped stones he bore.

"Uh—uh Nemicolopterus!" He held the bird-like fossil in his right hand. It was curled upon itself as if contained in an egg, the boney wings clearly enfolded around the ptero-saur's long tapered skull. "I've never seen a hatchling, not to mention an embryo!"

"Not many have," Bridget she agreed.

Hank raised his left hand, still shocked. "Mussaurus!" he whispered.

"Mouse Lizard" she translated and bristled. "Don't get me started. I would pay someone to empty my traps."

"Where did you get—"

"I have my sources," Bridget said and left it at that. Hank knew enough not to press. "Shall we talk business, professor?"

He raised a wary eye. "For….both…."

She quoted him a number.

Hank leaned back and made a face as if some rancid smell wafted into the room.

"How about, uh—" and countered with a figure.

"Umm," Bridget paused; she loved seeing the man squirm. "Sold."

They both shook hands and the Hank stuck the fossilized stones in his leather knapsack. He smiled at his purchases.

Hank reached in his right pocket and handed her a fat roll of bills. Bridget took the wad and dropped it in the right top desk drawer.

The sound of books falling off the shelf and hitting the floor caused both to look up.

"Sorry about that. You'll need to get some new bookends." He patted the contents of his knapsack. "Old ones, I mean" he corrected.

Bridget smiled. "Anything else I can do for you, sir?"

"That about covers it. You'll let me know of anything that comes in?"

"Of course. Pleasure doing business with you, Hank."

"Likewise," he turned for the door, stopped, looked back. "Bernhardt's, huh? I suppose it would be a great addition to the break room."

The Treasure of Freedom
by: Randall Lemon

One day, I woke up and my world had changed. In fact, it no longer was my world. It belonged to someone else, some "thing" else. Earth had been occupied by aliens. Not cute aliens like ET; frightening reptile-like beings. They looked like the velociraptors from "Jurassic Park," if someone had fed the raptors steroids.

These aliens were big and muscular with sharp teeth and razor claws. Each stood around eight feet tall. They used their tails more like bludgeons than whips. When I ventured onto the streets and saw them for the first time, I assumed I was dreaming. The aliens had occupied our world with a blitzkrieg Hitler would have envied. Military and police had been completely and easily neutralized. Our advanced weapons just refused to function. Only the most basic weapons could be used: rocks, clubs, knives, and our muscles and these Dinomen were much stronger. They were brutes; Goliaths to our Davids

Once we had been masters of our universe, now we were a slave society. More frightening than their size, was their attitude toward us. They had no fear of us; we just didn't matter. Mankind had become negligible in one week.

I saw one man stand up to the dinomen and he was literally pounded into the pavement by those huge tails. I had never been a brave woman, but that was certainly enough to cow me.

Like most of mankind, I gave in. If the military had proven ineffective, what could I possibly do? I walked the streets seeing horrible sights. The invaders were meat-eaters and we were their favorite entree. People were taken away from their families and found themselves chained to gurneys which stood next to tables covered with scalpels, bone saws and similar instruments.

Many people killed themselves, I thought of it myself. But I was too much of a coward. I started hiding in shadows when I went out to find food or see which friends were still alive.

One day I was coming down an alley near a familiar pawnshop. But something was different. The wall of the pawnshop had been "tagged" with bright neon paint. At first I could make no sense of the design, but then I realized that it was drawn in exaggerated Azteca style used by some Hispanic gangs. The longer I stared, the better I made out individual letters. Then I realized that these letters formed a picture within the words.

Hidden within the florid strokes of the gang graffiti were simple, direct messages like: "Ice the Invaders." "Rip the Reptiles." "Destroy the Dinos." and "Ax the Aliens." The letters whirled dizzyingly and if stared at long enough, a picture emerged of an alien with an ax separating his tail and head from the rest of his body. Blood geysered from the severed pieces of the creature.

I felt exhilarated. This artist was standing up for mankind. He was advocating defiance and preaching revolution through his words and pictures. Maybe hope was not gone. Maybe there were some people not ready to settle for extinction.

Over the next days, I found more examples of graffiti plastered around town. People I had known and loved all my life were disappearing. I couldn't take it anymore. I determined that as Dylan Thomas had advised, that I would "not go gentle into that good night. I would RAGE against the dying of the light."

I returned to the pawnshop where I had first found the graffiti, determined to find a way to join the revolution if there was one. I approached the doorway, above which hung three golden balls. A sign said "open," so I walked in.

A little man wearing wire-rimmed glasses stood behind the counter. He had tufts of wild, white hair bordering his bald pate. "Welcome to my store, "Trash to Treasure," how can I help you?"

I didn't know what to say, I felt stupid saying "point me to the revolution." So instead, I said, "I don't suppose you have any Azteca artwork like on the wall outside your store?"

The man appraised me a moment, "You sure it is that kind of art in which you are actually interested? It takes devotion and intense desire to immerse oneself in such a drastic style of art. It is not for the faint-hearted. And once one gives their heart to this particular art, there is no leaving until the collection is complete.

I took a deep breath and made my choice. "Whatever it takes, I'll find in myself. Complacency must give way to passion."

The pawnbroker reached below his counter and hit a button. A door near the back of the store swung open. "Take a look downstairs. I am sure I have what you're looking for there. I have a number of assistants who will be glad to help you." I realized the store was well-named. It was time to trade the trash of fear for the treasure of freedom!

City Business

by Patricia Lovett

Monday night's weekly meeting included the same angry and confused citizens. Arlene Grant turned to her husband Ed and said, "Bet me. The greedy fools will pass the store's expansion request. Bet me…"

Holding up his hand, Ed said, "I know they will Hon, I know they will," with impatience in his tobacco laced voice.

"The City Council meeting of Rose Town will come to order," the Presiding City Council President said as he pounded the gavel. At that moment, all eight Council members quieted their otherwise loud voices and obediently sat upright in their leather-like, plush seats.

Assuming her weekly routine, the city clerk adjusted her sparkly half-rimmed glasses and tucked her newly coiffed hair carefully behind her right ear. Sallie Anne Luck, the ever efficient City Clerk, ceremoniously performed roll call.

All answered with a response of 'Here' with the exception of Councilman Miser. He cheerfully answered, 'Present' as his shifty, beady eyes darted around the Council chamber looking for his business partner, Huncho. Laurel and Hardy, as they were often called behind their backs, had hatched a plan to get the Council to vote in favor on the expansion of their pawnshop.

They were already rubbing their greedy hands together, anticipating the adding of a loan component to their sleazy pawnshop. The new shop marquee board had already been ordered. The gaudy sign, in neon flashing lettering, read: Pay As You Can Loan Store.

Huncho's role in this little scheme had been to send each of the Council members a first class, round trip airline ticket to see the latest dinosaur exhibit in Palo Alto, California. The exhibit was a huge success for the State of California. Exhibit tickets were nearly impossible to acquire by legal means. There was still a 90-day wait time and the exhibit had been opened 9 months.

Rose Town had been in contention for the exhibit, but lost the bid by a narrow margin. The ruse was to make the City Council believe there would be a second exhibit built somewhere in the Country. Of course, all these thieves wanted was a yes vote on their newly designed, graffiti clad pawnshop.

'The Shop,' as it was known throughout Rose Town, was in a poor and rough part of town, which was represented by longtime resident Philipo.

"Councilmember Philipo", you vote for that corrupt bill and we'll vote you out!" That is what the Citizen's Complaint Board had told Philipo many times.

"We all know it and you know it too, an expansion of that sleazy place will be fertile ground for more crime."

"Get 'em to plant some grass and flowers around their existing store. Get them to hire reputable and reliable people," Christie, the pie maker had demanded.

"Whatta you think the chances of getting the required votes to pass the expansion?" Huncho has asked Miser several days before the meeting.

"Did you give them all their tickets"? the Councilman asked.

"Sure did", Huncho answered."And guess what?"

"What?" Miser responded.

"None of deem rascals turned down the free tickets. I think we got 'em.

"Just remember, when you come into the chamber tonight, don't sit near the front and don't try and talk to me. Ease in and ease out. I'll do the rest", Miser told Huncho.

After the roll call, the Clerk read the first item up for vote. Miser's heart started thumping. He already knew his request, or rather Huncho's request, was first on the docket.

"City Clerk, please read the first Request".

"Mr. Mayor, Request Number 98567 - request to expand 'The Shop'.

The Mayor looked up and down the Council's table. "All in favor of the expansion let it be know by raising your right hand".

The Clerk, counted the hands. "Seven in favor, Mr. Mayor.

The Mayor looked at Miser and gave him a single nod that said, 'well played.' Then in a strong voice he said "The request passes."

Huncho immediately got up and headed for the exit. "What's that smell"? He asked Christie as she entered the room.

"Smoke, sir. A building down the street's on fire."

As Huncho tried to exit the building, The City Clerk's voice boomed over the PA System. "Please exit the building. Do not take the elevator, I repeat, do not take the elevator. Take the stairs!"

* * *

Standing in the parking lot, Miser looked west, towards the store, and saw flames shooting skyward. He lost all hope the building could be saved.

With tears streaming down his face, Huncho started walking eastward. He never looked back.

Life Race

By Alli Vaughan

"Sylon, should we even be here?" Vendar asked me, his single-wheeled frame stooped in shadow. Only his glowing eyes peered from the dark.

"Sure why not?" I replied, ruffling my red plume of feathers like nothing bothered me.

I'd never been impressed with the city of Caron's underbelly. Sure the grime slunk around every gravel-marked corner and the stench caused my fingernails to recede into my nail beds, but it wasn't all that remarkable. Not to me. I'd lived in filth before.

Vendar's robotic gleam seemed out of place. His gears whined with embarrassment. "It's an awful place, I can't be seen here."

I bit back a laugh. Cyborgs were the last group needing to worry about what anyone thought of them. They'd traded their humanity thousands of years ago. "Just shut-up and let's get this over with."

I clutched an object to my chest, as if it were a prize, as we made our way to the Dead Man's Pawn Shop. Vendar didn't miss the action. "You know the metal rose is junk, it's not going to fetch you more than eight Drado's?"

I hope he missed that I flinched. "What's your point?"

"And that isn't going to be enough, is it Sylon?" Vendar sighed. "Not by half. And that is the last thing you own!"

Weight pressed inside my chest and blood rushed to my face. "No. No it isn't. But I have to try to get as much of the money I owe Wylan."

"Why bother? Why not ride in the race?" Vendar's voice bordered on pleading, but I know he was holding back.

"C'mon Vendar, you know I don't run from anything. And you know I don't, absolutely don't ride anymore. I'd rather die. And If Wylan's thugs are going to kill me anyway, at least I'll know I tried to pay my debts."

"Will you?" Vendar asked. "Will you actually know you did everything?" His eyes locked onto mine. I didn't reply.

"I didn't think so."

What else could I do though? Vendar didn't understand, I'd exhausted every resource, bled every friend dry, and still came up short. I sighed deeply and tried to distract myself as we plodded along.

The markings on the city walls bathed in the yellow-orange moonlight, caught my attention. My eyes traced the melted pinks, festering greens, all colors tagged by the poverty of this area. One design in particular made me forget for a moment that I'm basically a dead woman. "Look it's a dinosaur. But he's smiling."

"Why shouldn't he smile? They used to be extinct, you know?"

"You're kidding."

"Nope. Long before I traded flesh and bone for alloy and components, dinosaurs didn't exist. People used to dig up their bones and place them in museums. People didn't even know they could talk, thought they were dumb reptiles."

I frowned. "And now they wash windows and scrape a living off the underbelly of the world. Better they had remained a relic."

"They have families and lives, struggles and dreams like everyone."

"So. Why would they bother, being the scum of society?" I kicked a can and heard the clang as it struck the wall as we walked.

"They do have it hard, but anything is better than not existing, Sylon."

"Not existing..." Yes, I guessed that's what would happening to me soon.

"I see you are considering what will happen tomorrow when you come up short," Vendar said gently.

I shrugged.

"I hate seeing you like this. This isn't the Sylon I know. The fire-feathered woman, the flame-wrapped rider, she would have never given up on life like this."

"We can't all have immortality," the words left my mouth and I knew they'd sting. Vendar had paid for his immortal form with the last shred of his humanity.

The silence that followed confirmed that my words had stung. Regret strangled me and I wished I was already dead.

"Look, Sylon," Vendar began.

"Vendar, I'm so sorry."

"Stop. Listen, Sylon. You are like a little sister to me. I love you. I wish it didn't have to be like this. I wish there was another way. I would sell every inch of my metallic body if I thought...If I thought." Vendar must have wished in that moment that his body could pour tears.

"I'll do the race," I whispered. I bore no love for myself in that moment, but I did love that old scrap heap of metal before me more than I guessed I'd realized.

"You'll what?"

"You heard me. I'll enter the chopper race tonight. It's a better chance than anything else I've got. I swore I'd never ride again, but I am feeling phoenix fire and lucky. Besides the prize is double what I owe."

"I guess you're not going to become a relic, either," Vendar smiled.

I nodded. "Just like the dinosaurs. Back from the dead."

Dino Planetarium

by Sylvia Stein

It was Saturday and Danny awoke in a particularly great mood – his Dad, Jake, was taking him to the Dino Planetarium later. Danny loved everything there was about Dinosaurs, he was planning on becoming a paleontologist. He was only three years of age when his fascination with Dinosaurs had begun. It all started with a video his Dad had recorded; Danny would gladly watch it everyday if he could.

As Danny waited for his dad to come, he shuffled things back and forth on his desk. He came across a map in one of the drawers. Across the top of the map was written 'Dino Planetarium' and under that 'Map of The Island of Dinosaurs.' Danny got even more excited and began shouting out loud.

"Danny! What is it dear?" said his mother, Carol.

"Oh Mom you are not going to believe this!" he shouted, as he ran down the stairs, grasping the map. "Look at what I just found!"

"You are the lucky one," Carol said.

"I can't wait to show dad."

A wave of pain passed over Carol's face, but before Danny notices they both heard the car pulling up the driveway.

"Alright Danny, Dad's here now," Carol gave Danny a big hug, then let go of him so he could run to the door.

"Have fun," she called after him.

"I will," he said as the door slammed behind him.

Danny got in the car, but his dad couldn't get his seatbelt on.

"Sit still Danny. The longer this takes, the less time we'll have with the dinosaurs."

Danny stop moving, but his little body still quivered.

* * *

It felt like forever to Danny, but soon they arrived. Danny insisted that the run from the car and soon they stood in the central plaza. Danny's eyes darted from sight to sight.

Much too quickly, Danny said, "Look at all of the different Dinosaurs. And there, it looks like caveman graffiti. Aren't those the most amazing dinosaurs?"

"They sure are. Which is your favorite?"

"Albertosaurus. And the Brachiasaurus. And the T-Rex, too."

"No point having just one."

Danny wrapped his arms around his dad. "Thanks for bring me, Dad. You're the best."

Jake returned the hug and they started their adventure.

* * *

As they waited for a movie to start about flying dinosaurs, Danny took out his map and started studying it, looking for what to do next. Down in the corner, near the Jurassic Sea-life, he noticed an inscription:

To: Danny

Hope you enjoy your time the dinosaurs.

with love,

Mom

Danny smiled.

"Where'd you get the map? Did I buy it?"

"I got this from Mom."

"Well that was very nice of her."

"Yes, it was. She likes to surprise me."

"You know, you're pretty lucky to have her." Jake smiled.

"That's what she says about you," echoed Danny.

Jake sighed.

After the movie, sky tram, Fight for Survival, lunch, King's of the Jungle, In all Sizes, and of course, Jurassic Sea-life, it was time to leave. Danny pouted and walked slowly as they headed towards the exit.

"Now Danny, please don't be sad."

"I know, Dad." Danny forced a little smile. "But, I just miss you when you're not around."

"Me too." Jack pulled Danny close as they walked.

"Hey! Remember in two weeks you are out of school and you'll be spending a couple of weeks with me."

"I can't wait." Danny started skipping.

"Me neither." Jake started skipping, too.

"Oh, and Dad, they have a new presentation opening in a couple of weeks. Can you bring me back.

"I'd love that, Danny."

* * *

Danny didn't stop talking about all the things they had seen until they pulled up to Danny's mom's house. Danny got out of the car and ran to his mother.

"Mom! I had the best time. I can't wait to tell you all about it!" He threw his arms around her.

"I'm so glad hunny."

"And mom, thanks for the map." Danny released his mom and ran into the house.

Carol gave a little jump when she looked up and saw Jake standing there.

"I. I just wanted to tell you. Danny had a great time," he said and smiled.

"Oh, I'm so glad. I knew he would."

"So, Danny said there's a new exhibit opening in a few weeks. And …"

"Sure, you can take him."

"No. I was wondering. Well, would you like to come with us?"

"I'd love to." Carol smiled, an honest and for real smile.

"Well. Then. I'll see you later." Jake turned and left.

As Danny got ready for bed, he couldn't help but grin. It made him feel special knowing that both of his parents wanted to make him happy, and as all children, he had no idea how special he made his parents feel.

An Empty Box of Treasure

by Rejoice Denhere

I woke up one morning feeling sad. I figured it was because of my nocturnal wanderings, but I couldn't recall my dream. I was still thinking about what could be bringing me down, other than my non-existent back balance, when I got on the bus to work. In the back of the bus sat a man sleeping whom I had nicknamed 'Sleeping Man'. I would have bet he was having good dreams.

I left work early that evening. I needed the extra money, but I just couldn't shake the feeling that had been with me all day. On the bus home I closed my eyes and tried to remember my dream. I must have fallen asleep, because all of a sudden I sensed that someone was standing over me. When I opened my eyes, wouldn't you know it, Sleeping Man was staring at me. Apparently he wasn't happy I'd taken his seat.

I moved and he nodded to me with satisfaction as he sat down. I noticed that he was carrying a small wooden box.

I said, "I have a small wooden box similar to yours. Mine's made of oak with a dinosaur on the lid."

"Really?" he said. "My friend, John, he owns a pawn shop, well, he collects them. I should introduce you to him."

At that moment I remembered the end of my dream.

"You're wealthy Lizzie," my father had said.

Considering how broke I was, there's no wonder I'd woken up feeling sad. My eyes welled up with tears, which I wiped away. With concern in his voice sleeping man asked if I was okay. Overwhelmed by emotion I told him about my father.

"… and when he died he left me nothing," I finished sobbing.

"What kind of a father…"

"Actually," I cut in, "he left me the wooden box."

"Really?" he said. "You should come see John."

I couldn't help smiling. "Thank you Mr …"

"Name's Tim," he replied.

We arranged to visit John that Saturday.

* * *

We took a different bus to a part of town I didn't know. The walls were sprayed with graffiti, the bins were overflowing and the pavement was littered with rubbish. Warning bells started ringing in my head as we walked down the deserted street. Tim, if that was his real name, could be a con-artist – or worse. I breathed deep and tried to calm my nerves.

With relief, we reached the pawn shop. Its windows were dirty, the door squeaked and the inside was as dimly lit as a bar. My hands were sweating when I handed the box to John. He looked at it, turning it over and read the inscription inside.

"Is it worth anything?" I asked.

"Depends." He hummed. "I'd give you twenty-five for it, but, if your know its secret, I'm sure its worth a lot more."

I told John that my father had given it to me, and that he had made me learn a rhyme that went with it.

"Seem like your father had strong traditional values. Fortunately for you, I'm sort of an expert. The dinosaur on the lid here, it symbolizes wealth which predators desire. The rhyme on the inside is the clue to locating the wealth. Only if you know the full rhyme can you find it.

* * *

We left after that. I almost sold the box to John, heaven knows I needed the twenty-five, but my dad's rhyme kept repeating in my head. I remembered him telling me, "Keep it safe. When I'm gone follow the instruction in the rhyme I taught you." I also remembered ignoring my father's words.

The following Monday I went to the bank. I sat in bank manager's office feeling both stupid and nervous. He was probably going to think I was crazy. He checked my identity and looked at the box.

"Do you know the rest of the rhyme," he asked?

"… Saved beneath the arch for daddy's girl. Wealth like his love, like a pearl."

The manager smiled and nodded. When I had turned ten, my dad bought me some property and opened a bank account into which rent proceeds were paid.

I really was wealthy all this time. I had just forgotten how much I was loved.

Of Dinosaurs and Girls

by Laura Stafford

The grayed picnic table was smooth along the edges from the backs of a thousand legs sitting upon it's aging wood. Lily ran her fingers along the deep furrows that marked old loves and proclamations - "I was here," "Joe loves Megan," "Led Zeppelin," "Class of '74."

The familiar grain spelled out her own name: Lily Loves Jordan.

She should have know then how precarious it was to stand on the edge of the love cliff, reaching out to someone who didn't love as much. It wasn't Jordan that carved this dedication to joining souls, it had been Lily.

All Lily knew then was her love ran deep, like a canyon, carving out a ravine that she wanted Jordan to fill with love and passion.

How silly it all seemed now, sitting here on the worn picnic table of her childhood, sorting memories from not so long ago, that she embraced naivety and delusions as reality, and let her reality flounder so recklessly.

At 23-years-old, with a son on his way to kindergarten, Lily felt old and tired.

Evan came running to the picnic table, sweaty and breathless. "Will I learn about dinosaurs at school?" he asked.

"Yes baby," Lily told him. Lily had been talking to him all summer about school, but with this last week of summer coming to a close, he was getting nervous, asking more questions.

Tomorrow they would be meeting his new teacher.

* * *

Mrs. Delaney had hard eyes, but a soft, smiling mouth. She talked to Evan and then turned her attention to Lily, who squirmed in the kindergartener-sized chair. Although the conversation proved cordial, Lily felt like she was under attack. She spoke defensively, trying to prove that she was a good mom, even though her job at the deli paid barely enough to feed the kid, she had pawned everything of value at Mastin's Gold and Pawn down on 7th street, and she was thanking God her mother still let her live at home.

Of course, how could Mrs. Delaney know any of that, or be judging her for it? But still, there was a raw feeling in the pit of Lily's stomach.

* * *

At dinner, she told her mom, "Why should I be jealous of her? It's not like she's pretty or something,"

Her mother laughed. "Child, everything in life is not about looks. It's not even about love, despite what all them books say. You're jealous cause there's a hole in your spirit. And when you look about you, you can see people who are whole, and that's what you want for yourself."

"So what is it then? What is it that makes you whole?" Lily wondered.

"Oh! I can't tell you what makes you whole. There might not be any one single thing - maybe it's a combination of things, a mixture, a recipe for wholeness..." Lily's mother looked off into the distance.

"Are you whole?"

"Yes, I think I am. I miss your father of course, but I'm content with my memories and the time that God gave us together... Do you want to know what it was that made me whole?"

"Yes!" Lily responded quickly.

"Painting," her mother answered matter-of-factly, setting her jaw. Her mother was still young, Lily noticed now, only 47-years-old, smooth-skinned and regal in her demeanor. Refined, wise, and a survivor, raising two kids on a meager amount after their father passed away in a trucking accident.

"Really? Painting?"

"Yup. Painting... See, when I was young, I wanted to be a mom. A wife. Nothing more than that. And when I met your father, I was sure that was my life. But when he died, not only did I need money, I needed something to do. Something to do with my hands..." She looked at her hands now, barely wrinkled, but showing a bit of age in their calloused palms and dry knuckles. She rubbed them together and then clapped them once, making a slap that startled Evan and made them all laugh.

"These hands," she continued with a shrug, "were restless. So I joined the painting crew, and the guys liked me, and I liked the painting. And I worked my way up from part-time when you kids were young and now I have my own crew. I did that. These hands did that."

Lily looked at her own hands.

"Lily," her mother covered Lily's hands with her own older, yet matching pair. "What can your hands do?"

Boredom

By by D. C. Mills

We were bored.

Bored.

Bored.

Bored.

There was no proper work to be found – and mind you, by this time we were not picky. There was, of course, the one job you can always get in a port; but we had promised each other to never ever get that desperate. After all, we did always eat.

But with next to no money, there was precious little fun to be had. We were down to spray painting bright yellow smiley faces on walls, fences, any surface that would take it, and using them for target practice. Alex got the idea, as usual. And I went along, as usual.

The cops didn't seem to mind that we shot up random buildings. They made no effort to find, let alone catch, us. Pity, really: that would have added some spice to the game. As it was, we spent our days and half the nights drifting through the dusty space port, looking for odd jobs and target areas.

Bored.

Which was why we, one evening just after sundown, found ourselves outside the little pawn shop in a nameless backstreet. I had been afraid of the owner, old Murphy, when I was a kid, and truth be told, I still was. But no way was I letting Alex see that.

"Wanna go in?"

"Why not? Might kill half an hour."

The old man behind the reinforced ceramic glass had shrunk in the years since we had been here last. He had also somehow lost his scariness.

"Good evening," he greeted us with professional friendliness. "Now, what can I do for you young – sters," he quickly adjusted his words before blundering into any gender-specific appellation.

"We're looking for a present," Alex said.

While chatting, we strolled around the shop. Shelves from floor to ceiling were stacked with strange and curious objects from all over the galaxy and beyond. All of them were treasures in their own right, but all of them had been deemed less important than other, more immediate needs.

It made me sad to think that people had given up these wonderful things for ready cash to hand over to sellers of instant pleasures. Or maybe medics. Even grocers.

"I can"t help but notice," old Murphy said, "the two of you are so very alike. Have you had any – work – done to become so?"

"Nope," I said, "we're natural born twins."

"We've always been like this,"Alex added.

"Very rare," he said musingly. "Very rare indeed."

We were used to being seen as specimens and not bothered by it anymore. Natural twins had become exceedingly rare; though we were not, as I had claimed, quite natural. On the other hand, we had been born together and identical.

We were indeed specimens, results of a now abandoned genetic experiment. Someone had deemed other work more important than the likes of us.

"Look at this," Alex said. A metal box, lid embossed with intricate symbols.

"We have to buy this," I said without knowing why. I only knew we needed this box, and Alex knew it, too.

We went over to old Murphy. "How much?"

The old man looked at us and at the box, as if he had never seen it before or had forgotten its existence. "That box," he said finally in a faraway voice, "has been sitting on its shelf for many, many years. But I remember the day and the man who came in with it. He was at his wits end. He didn't even want money for it. I think he just wanted to be rid of it."

He looked at us sharply. "What do you guys want with it, eh? Do you know its true value?"

We exchanged a glance, Alex and I. We each knew what the other was thinking.

"Nah," I said in an offhand tone, "just an old box. We thought it might be pretty, that's all."

"If it was dusted off and polished up a bit," Alex added.

"But if you don't want to sell," I continued.

"We'll be out of here," Alex finished.

"Of course I want to sell," the old man grumbled. "Only you surprised me. Nobody's given that old box the time of day ever since it came in here."

We waited while he estimated what price to ask, aware that he had revealed not having paid much for it.

In the end, we got the box for almost all we had. We took it out of the pawn shop, into the field beyond the perimeter fence. After some searching, we found a key hidden in a slit underneath the bottom of the box. Inside was a complicated mechanism.

"It's a music box!"

We had had one once, long ago. This one was old, though, and rusty. It didn't work.

"Something"s stuck, I think," I said, fiddling with it.

"Oh, never mind. Let's go shoot something."

Alex was always the impatient one.

"No, I think I've got it now – look!"

What came out of the box was not music, but light. Brilliant light in all the colours of the rainbow and more beamed up from the mechanism, like a holo-projector.

The light intensified, glittered, overwhelmed us.

All at once, a creature appeared out of the light. A big, scary reptile, with huge teeth.

Not a hologram.

It attacked Alex, ripping flesh and crushing bones. I tried to shoot it, but I was shaking too much to aim.

Then the light folded in on itself, taking the creature with it. I blinked in the sudden darkness.

"Alex."

"Alex?"

"Alex!"

Nothing.

* * *

You know the rest.

Finally, the cops took an interest. I was arrested, tried, convicted.

Nobody believed my story: the portal box refused to work again – maybe its battery had only had juice left for one go.

The media, of course, loved it, as they love all failed experiment.

"TWIN SLAYS TWIN."

And here I am. In an institution for the criminally insane. Talking to you.

The Trinity

By Gene Hilgreen

My hands and face bore the marks of my trade. I was homeless, and trying to clean the stink of the street off my body. Water cascaded down my chest, as I splashed it from the sink basin to my face and body. Above the sink, morning rays of sunlight glared off the mirror. I didn't want to look, but was drawn to the image—it was majestic. Old Glory, the tattoo on my chest appeared to wave.

It was going to be a good day.

Last night was not, it rained hard, and neighborhood kids beat me in my sleep. They trashed my house—the cardboard box I lived it.

I'll get another house today.

The bells on the church began to chime, it was six, and the mass would start in fifteen minutes. The priest was a good man, especially for the street people—he let us wash up, and he fed us every Friday night. I knew he wouldn't say so, but he didn't want us scaring his congregation away. I would be gone before mass started. I gathered my worldly assets; my bush hat, Camo jacket and three blankets—it was time to find breakfast.

It was going to be a good day.

I wasn't always like this; there was a time, when I had a great job and a family. That all ended after nine-eleven—I snapped.

"Get a job, you bum," said the passerby.

"Have a good day," I said and picked up my tip bucket, there was a folded twenty at the bottom.

It was going to be a good day.

"Thank you," I said, it's time to go to work.

My spot was the block between Little Italy and the beginning of China Town. The buildings were covered in graffiti, but the pawn shop two doors down—drew a unique clientele. I laid out one of my blankets and set my tip bucket out. I hung my wet Camo on the hook that I had fashioned into the wall months ago.

I slipped on my bush hat, and the only dry clothing I had—my worn out, Property United States Marine Corps, red T-shirt with the Bulldog mascot. Now on duty, I smiled at my first customer.

"Semper Fi," he said, and threw a buck in my bucket.

At noon, not counting the twenty, I made nineteen dollars and sixty-nine cents—the year I went to Nam. There was a pizza place around the corner, the owner sold slices to passerby's. I got three slices and was content. On my way back to my spot, I saw a black limo parked in front of the pawnshop. A man in a dark suit was standing by the rear passenger door. As I approached, he opened the door, and a well dressed man stepped out—he approached me.

"Semper Fi, Gunny," he said.

"Semper Fi," I said. "How do you know I'm a Gunny, do I know you?"

"I would hope so," he said. "But, I saw your jacket."

"What can I do for you—"

"The three bones in your bush hat are of great interest to me. Where did you find them?"

"I was with the First of the First, in Quang Tri in 1969."

"Who has the others," he said?

"Whoa, hold on a second. Who are you?"

"I'm Buck Davidssen, Jameson's younger brother."

"Holy ****! Jameson was my Marine buddy, my closest friend—I trusted him with my life."

"He trusted his life with you, and talked about you all the time in his letters home. Continue."

"We were on patrol and digging in for the night, when I found six bones. I gave him three and I kept three. We put them in our hats for luck. The Holy Trinity; the Father, the Son and the Holy Spirit."

"I saw you at his funeral," Buck said. "You stood in the back, why didn't you come by?"

"I felt responsible," Gunny said. "I shipped out three weeks before he was killed. I couldn't live with myself."

"When his body was shipped home, three bones were among his belonging. I had them checked out by experts."

"What kind of fish are they from?"

"Gunny, those are not teeth. They are horns, from a baby Triceratops and they're worth millions.

"You just made my day. I knew when I woke up; it was going to be a great day."

"Come with me to the pawn shop. The proprietor collects dinosaur bones. It's time that you got your life back together."

The proprietor's smile beamed, when we entered the shop, he spread his arms, when he saw my hat.

"Welcome to my humble establishment, I'm about to change your life."

Expressing Ourselves

By Douglas G. Clarke

I don't know how I got tangled up in the mess, but I know I never intended to. Was it my sister and her persistent urging to take her shopping? My mother's nagging to get a job and do something with my life? Maybe it was my absent father's lack of guidance. Maybe it was just me.

In any case, it started one afternoon in a alley. My friends and I were "expressing" ourselves. It's not like we were hurting anyone, what's one more layer of paint on the top of twenty others. But that's not the way the cops saw it. They tackled two of my friends as we scattered like cockroaches. I was lucky I guess, I made it home.

Of course the second I stepped through the door the two women in my life were all over me - mom questioning me about my job search and Maria wanting me to play chauffeur. It doesn't happen very often, but they came to an agreement – take Maria shopping and apply for jobs at the stores we visited. Now, I can hold myself against one of them, but against two? Well I got cleaned up, my cheek tweaked by my mom, and Maria and I were off.

Our third stop was at the "Cash for Stuff" pawnshop. Maria was looking for a necklace to wear to the prom and what better place to look for that non-necessity than where people go when the necessities rear their heads. The place was crammed from floor to ceiling with stuff. I heard once that the difference between stuff and junk is that junk has value. i.e. junk yards. From the looks of it, that saying was right - this stuff was worthless.

I decided to wait outside, while my sister looked at the display cases full of shiny things, leaning against the wall. The sounds of traffic were all around me. The last thing I was expecting was the angry yell of a cop. That is, of course, what I heard.

I opened my eyes while I listened too his footfalls approaching. I suppose I could have run, I beat him before, but my sister was inside and my mom's car was parked at the curb. I stood there, trying to act cool, like maybe he wasn't yelling at me. It didn't work. I felt the handcuff encircle my left wrist and then I was spinning around so that my face was against the wall.

That, of course, is when Maria walked out. I wanted to tell her to calm down. I heard her yelling and her fists hitting the cops back. But all I could do was grunt as my face was pressed harder into the wall. I didn't see what happened next, but from the screaming back and forth I figured it out.

Maria pulled out her phone and started recording my arrest. The cop didn't take favorably to this and in an effort to keep things under control slid me down to the sidewalk.

Maria started screaming again when she saw that some of my face was smeared along the wall. The cop really didn't like this turn of events and pressed his knee in my back as he tried to grab Maria's phone.

Maria backed away and yelled something about the cop having brontosaurs breath. The cop gave up on her and decided the best thing to do was to get out of there. He yanked me to my feet and pushed me down the street, Maria yelling behind us.

I could tell you that getting finger printed and photographed was no big deal, or that my mom wasn't upset when a cop dropped Maria off at home, car still outside the pawnshop. I could even tell you that my street cred went up with my blood stain on the wall. But none of that would be true.

Truth is, it scared me. I thought I was going to die or end up some convict's play thing. I ended up doing 40 hours of community service – painting over graffiti with gray paint. And go figure, the guy at the pawnshop liked the way I worked and gave me a job. Now my mom's happy that I've got a job, Marie keeps using my 10% discount, and my dad, well he still not around, but he is having a little more influence on me – I know I don't want to end up a piece of trash like him.

After Words

Unexpected Treasure
Harry Alexiou

The fact that many of us spend too much energy trying to gain physical wealth is a reflection of society in the 21st century. Without good health, happiness in your heart and the love of close family we have nothing. Through a child's eyes things take on different meaning, perception is altered; the worthless dinosaur figurine had more value to Tommy than money ever could. Omnipresent advertising raises desire creating a society which wants more than it can afford; did we need all those gadgets tucked in a drawer at home? Did we need all those 'optional extras' on that new car? Did we need a five bedroom home when a three would suffice? Sure it's great to have 'stuff' but it shouldn't be an all consuming ambition. One item with sentimental value is worth more than a thousand with none. Appreciate the simple things in life, look at what you have, not that what you do not. Aim high, but take a measured approach and live within your means; the desire for material possessions, with short 'feel-good' expiry dates, is self perpetuating.

What Becomes
Tim Girard

This was a fun story to write. It gave me an opportunity to tap into the deep darkness of every man. Truth be told, this is not a story about every man. In fact, try this out: go back and re-read the story. Think about a big lumbering T-Rex this time. Then give thought to the every man darkness, the despair of just scraping through a day.

3 D T. C.
Mike Boggia

Tagging and street art are two different expressions by young artists driven by contrasting ideas and ideals. The murals painted have always attracted me and set my mind to wondering about the person or persons behind the paintings.

What if the artist, T. C., has more than an artistic talent? The thought of blending magic and art, including a dinosaur, played out in my mind. Both subjects have been of interest since childhood and were combined for this story.

I hope you enjoyed it.

Dragon Bones
Joseph Scott Amis

Dragon Bones continues a series of short stories that incorporate principal characters and the medieval settings and themes from To Shine With Honor, my three-volume novel of the First Crusade.

These short stories represent a conscious effort to take these elements into an alternate direction, with the aspects of supernatural horror and fantasy brought into an accurate historical setting.

The characters, knights Thierré and Galien de Coudre, as well as their younger sister Alisende, have been recast as eleventh-century hunters of all types of apparitions, including zombies, dragons, vampires, and witches; also as detectives who seek to discover truth and bring to justice those who would misuse dangerous occult forces to gain wealth, power, and position.

A historical note for Dragon Bones: Var is an actual place in France, located approximately as described in the story and known since ancient times. It is noted for the extensive deposits of dinosaur remains excavated there.

The Birthday Present
A.A. Abbott

This bittersweet tale was written after a visit to the northern port city of Newcastle in England. As in much of the north, the decline of heavy industry in the U.K. has left poverty in its wake. A life on state benefits (the dole) is all that lies ahead for many men and women of working age. Still, when I saw brand new and boxed children's toys in the window of a pawnshop just before Christmas, I wondered at the desperation that had caused would-be proud present-givers to bring them there.

The area is close knit, with a rich dialect all its own. I have taken elements ("bairn", a word also used in Scotland to mean 'child', and "Me mam"), but largely used conventional English in order to keep the story accessible. I hope it captures the humour and resourcefulness of this still beautiful, but deprived, British city.

Baby Rose
Lynette White

Set in an environment far too many us are familiar with, I introduce Rose Cassidy. A single mom plagued with misfortune, but determined to rise above it. Forced to sell her treasures to take care of her most precious treasure, her son.

Unbeknownst to Rose she had an escape. What would you do if you learned you had a talent that could change your entire future?

As writers we all hope we write that one story that will make us millions. Personally, I prefer to make my fortune one thought provoking story at a time. I challenge myself to write my passion for life into every story I create. This is not meant to be a sad story, but a story of renewed hope.

Bookends
Allen Quintana

Now and then a story comes out on a person finding some antique with a famous or infamous history. A death mask of some notable, or a lost silent movie, or some such turns up in an overlooked antique store, or a barn, or literally a hole in the wall that the artifact was tagged with tape for $5 then suddenly is priceless.

The search never gets old no matter how old the find is.

Folks who frequent these places want to be surprised. They're of a mind that whatever old fossil it is, they stopped looking for it long ago because it seems that's when the thing shows up. And when that prize is in your hands, on comes your best poker-face so as not to clue the proprietor that your treasure will go for a ransom rather than the song you hope for. If the store owner knows what is had, it's time to dicker.

Everybody happy.

The Treasure of Freedom
Randall Lemon

The United Sates is a land based on the concept of revolution. Our forefathers wanted fair treatment from the government of England and when they realized they would never get it, they joined together to fight for their freedom so they could establish a new government of their own.

Back in the days of Washington, Franklin and Jefferson the artistic expression of political ideals found their way into an art form called the pamphlet. Writers like Thomas Paine were as important to the revolution as the guns carried by Washington's soldiers. Today, artistic expression of political ideals often appears as graffiti on the walls of buildings in our cities.

Given the required elements of dinosaurs, graffiti and a pawn shop, the first thing that flashed in my mind was the TV series "V" which first appeared as a mini series in 1983 which although it was cheesy by modern standards was one of my favorite at the time.

If one day, we turned around and our precious freedom was gone what would we, the average citizen do? Would we rally to defend our rights? And who would be our generals in this struggle? This is the idea I wanted to explore in my story.

City Business
Patricia Lovett

A citizen's participation in the political process is both an honor and a privilege. As one has often heard… all politics is local. Honesty is required in order to make our government work effectively and efficiently. Whenever dishonesty is present, it is a financial burden on both citizens and other governments.

While City Business is characterized by wit, charm and absurdity, the overall theme of the story rings true. Voters expect campaign promises to be honored and integrity to be the order of the day. However, all too often, these human elements are nowhere to be found, after an election.

Life Race
Alli Vaughan

Most of my writing is fantasy, but sometimes I like to dabble in science fiction. For this piece a Cyborg is one of the main characters, the best friend and guardian to the protagonist. The main character is sort of the reluctant hero. This would make a fun piece as a larger book and its something I've kicked around.

Dino Planetarium
Sylvia Stein

This is the story of young Danny and how he looks forward to going to spend time with his father at the Dino Planetarium.

This outing is special for young Danny because both of his parents are no longer together.

It is a short story that shows how two parents try to maintain a united front to make life less complicated for the love of their son.

I hope you enjoyed this story.

An Empty Box of Treasure
Rejoice Denhere

An Empty Box of Treasure is written in honour of anyone who has ever been broke and wished they could receive an inheritance but never did. It is also written for anyone who has ever been disappointed at being given a seemingly useless gift.

Yes, some of us wish for a financial windfall which will allow us to leave our dreary jobs and spend long days in the warm sun surrounded by beautiful people. That includes me!

Sadly, it doesn't always happen. Even on those rare occasions when we are fortunate enough to either receive an inheritance or be given a gift, it may appear to be of little or no value at all.

Before you dismiss any gift as worthless, look again because it may just contain hidden treasure. Like the main character in this story I have proved this to be true in my own life.

Of Dinosaurs and Girls
Laura Stafford

Of Dinosaurs and Girls was written as an experiment of looking at a woman in transition. The story does not focus on her life before or after her major decision was made, but on the few unsure moments of her actual conversion.

The main character is on the cusp of a realization, on the verge of something better. All she needs is the final push - which comes from her mother's story. Wondering what her hands can do gives her the power to begin exploring the possibilities.

Boredom
by D. C. Mills

Writing with required elements can be challenging.

For this story, they were graffiti and a dinosaur.

And a pawnshop had to be included in the setting.

So, how do you bring those elements together?

This is where the fun begins.

The setup allows the writer to focus or not focus on the required elements: they can be central to the story, or passed by on the periphery. I like to, whenever possible, include an element without naming it directly.

When the elements are given, I let them simmer for a while in my mind, so they can present various possibilities.

Then, at some point, the first line decides to show up, and the story can begin.

The Trinity
by Gene Hilgreen

The Writers 750 Group, run by Heather Schultz, was a Godsend to me. It gave me the chance to hone my writing skills while interacting with other members—who are now like family—on a wide range of topics.

It also gave me the chance to experiment, have some fun. The theme and required criteria for The Trinity, allowed me to create a new character, and draw on situations from my past. It was the third short story I had ever written, and was chosen the favorite for the contest.

Gunny Bob would later play prominently in my Buck Axele Davidssen series.

I hope you enjoyed it

Expressing Ourselves
Douglas G. Clarke

I struggled with the disparate highlights in this months prompt. They all cried out for superficial descriptions, but I wanted to write something that dealt with the human condition.

I settled on a story about a young man or woman who's life was metaphorically trash and an event that helped turn it around.

Though never named in the story, I came to like this young person in the short 740 words of the story. I can't say I understand their situation or how their interactions with their family would truly effect them, but something in this person speaks to me.

Thank you for reading *Trash to Treasure*, we hope you enjoyed it. If you would like to find out more about the book and its authors, please visit www.agoodtale.com

Also, look for our other books
  Violet Hopes
  Of Past and Future